BLOOMSBURY CHILDREN'S BOOKS
Bloomsbury Publishing Plc
50 Bedford Square, London, WC1B 3DP, UK
29 Earlsfort Terrace, Dublin 2, Ireland

BLOOMSBURY, BLOOMSBURY CHILDREN'S BOOKS and the Diana logo are
trademarks of Bloomsbury Publishing Plc

First published in Great Britain 2021 by Bloomsbury Publishing Plc

Text copyright © Katrina Charman 2021
Illustrations copyright © Nick Sharratt 2021

A catalogue record for this book is available from the British Library

ISBN: HB: 978 1 5266 0338 8 • PB: 978 1 5266 0339 5 • eBook: 978 1 5266 03401

2 4 6 8 10 9 7 5 3 1
Printed and bound in China by Leo Paper Products, Heshan, Guangdong

All papers used by Bloomsbury Publishing Plc are natural, recyclable products
from wood grown in well managed forests. The manufacturing
processes conform to the environmental regulations of the country of origin

To find out more about our authors and books visit
www.bloomsbury.com and sign up for our newsletters

For Brick, Piper and Riley – K.C.

For Julie, Vanessa, Lara
and the Book Nook – N.S.

Rumble, Rumble, Dinosaur

Katrina
Charman

Nick
Sharratt

BLOOMSBURY
CHILDREN'S BOOKS
LONDON OXFORD NEW YORK NEW DELHI SYDNEY

Rumble, rumble, DINOSAUR!
Wake up dinos near and far.

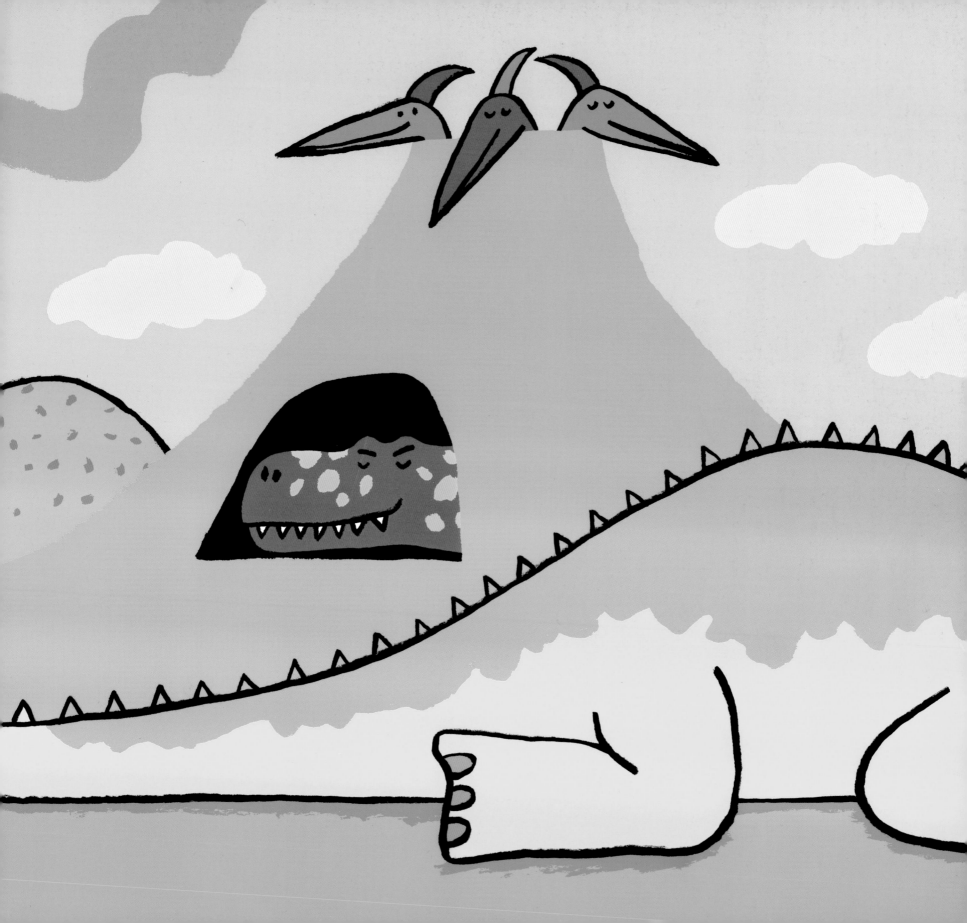

Swish your tails and
stretch your wings,
let's see what the
new day brings.

Rumble, rumble,
DINOSAUR!
Wake up dinos near and far.

Pterodactyls flying high,
watch them as they ZOOM on by.

Laughing, playing with their friends,
dino fun-time never ends.

Munch
and crunch
above the trees,
Diplodocus eating
leaves.

STOMPING! STAMPING! with large feet, the tallest dino you will meet.

Munch and crunch above the trees, reaching for the highest leaves.

CLOMP! and CRASH!
Then FLICK! and WHACK!
Stegosaurus clears a track.

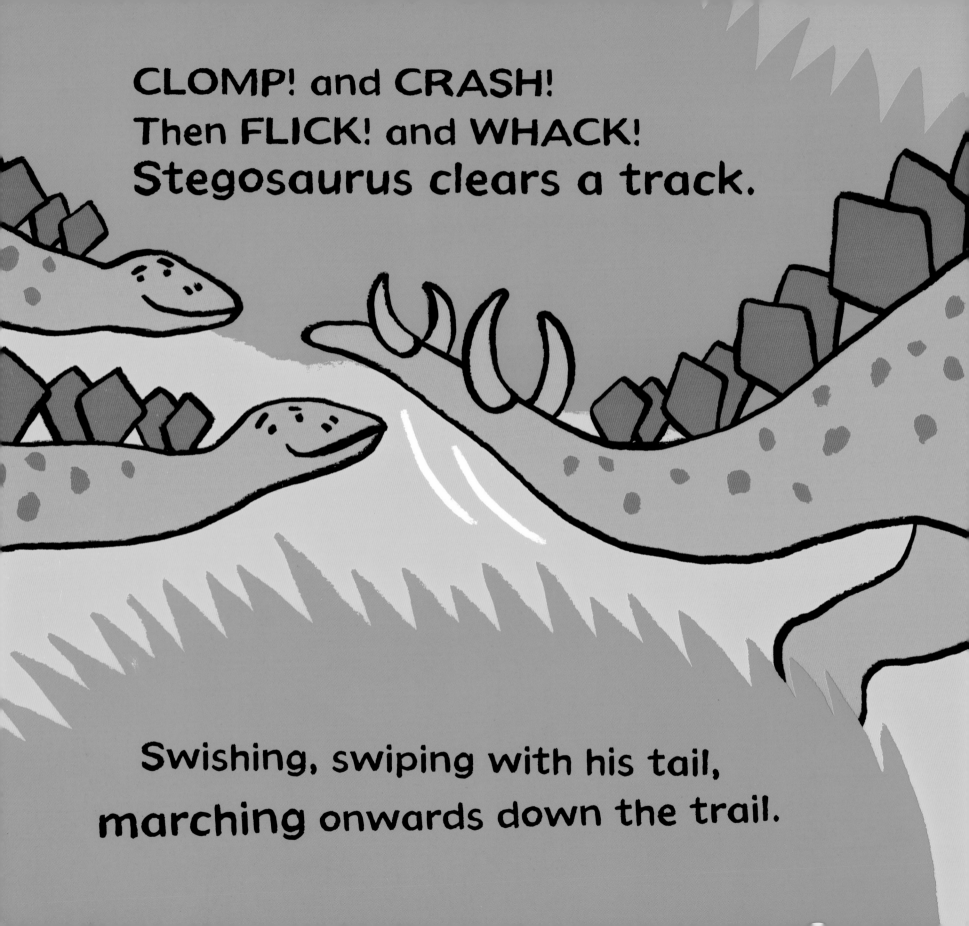

Swishing, swiping with his tail,
marching onwards down the trail.

CLOMP!
and **CRASH!**
along the track,
Stegosaurus
leads his pack.

SPLISHING! SPLASHING! in the sea,
searching for some fish for tea.

Kronosaurus gliding past,
with her flippers she's so fast.

SPLISHING! SPLASHING! in the sea, ducking, diving, wild and free.

Tromping, tramping
in the sun,
triceratops have
lots of fun.

Three sharp horns
and snapping beaks,
playing up and down the peaks.

Tromping, tramping
in the sun,
triceratops have lots of fun!

Sneaking, creeping,
leap and bounce,
velociraptors
hunt and **POUNCE!**

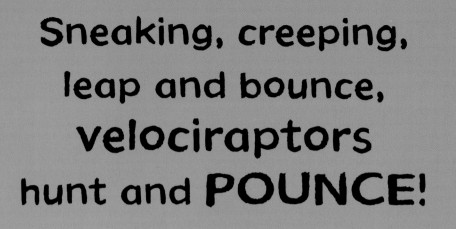

They work
together as a team,

hiding where
they can't be **seen.**

Sneaking, creeping, leap and bounce,
velociraptors chase and POUNCE!

Growling, prowling, thunder **ROAR!**
Who's this **scary** dinosaur?

Watch out!
T-Rex races by –
careful not to catch
her eye!

Growling, prowling,
thunder **ROAR!**
She's the **fiercest**
dinosaur.

Swooping, stomping, sprinting beasts,
heading for their dino feast.

Chewing leaves and chomping meat,
so much tasty food to eat!

Swooping, stomping, sprinting beasts, gobbling down their dino feast.

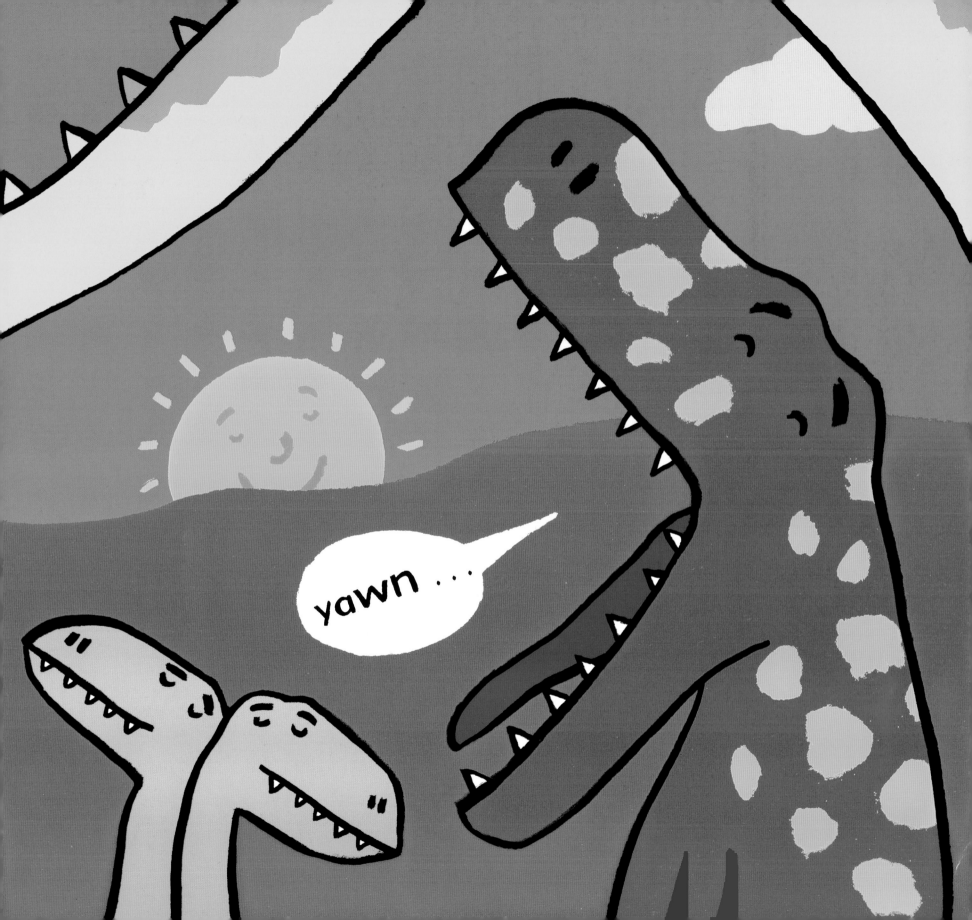